The Wolves Crescent

Nomusa Madlala

ISBN 978-93-5610-831-8

Published in India 2022 by Pencil

A brand of
One Point Six Technologies Pvt. Ltd.
123, Building J2, Shram Seva Premises,
Wadala Truck Terminal, Wadala (E)
Mumbai 400037, Maharashtra, INDIA
E connect@thepencilapp.com
W www.thepencilapp.com

CONTENTS

Chapter 1

Sarah Cooper was getting her little sister, Zoey ready for school. After she had run the bath, woken her up, and helped her get dressed, She had made her favorite chocolate chip pancakes and a glass of milk. As she was upstairs combing her lustrous, thick otherwise black hair, she spotted a photo of her parents which sat on the bedside table of her room. Then suddenly, flashes of the accident began to materialize in her head. That cold, night. The car screeching, before tumbling over and hurdling across the road. She tried to shake the memory out of her head as a tear ran down her cheek. Sarah! Sarah! She could hear something call her name but at the same time, it was absolutely quiet. She turned to see Zoey standing in the doorway, calling her name repeatedly. We're going to be late. She said, arms crossed. Sarah displayed a smile before getting up from the bed, grabbing her backpack, and going down the stairs. Aren't you going to eat? Zoey asked as they stepped out onto the front porch. Nah, I'll probably eat later. Sarah said, taking her sister's hand as they walked down the street. Since her parents were not around anymore, Sarah had to look after her sister. She had to feed her, bathe her and take her to school every morning. The leaves rustled and a bird landed on the branch of a tree as Sam's head jerked up reflexively. When he saw it was only a bird, he relaxed. He stood beneath a pine tree, in wolf form looking at a dead deer he had just killed. After devouring half of the deer, he licked at his gums and lips painstakingly, to make sure there was no stain on them, before turning back into a human. Deep in the woods, where no one would see him, he'd come to hunt and feed. The sunlight filtered down onto his hair. In jeans and a T-shirt, Sam Abbott looked exactly like a normal high school student. But he wasn't, he was a wolf. A large brown wolf. He heard a howl in the distance, then a grey wolf appeared. Sam, what are you doing here? It said, transforming into a human. I was hungry, I wanted a little snack. Sam wiped his mouth with the back of his hand after turning back into a human. Well, we're going to be late for school. Damien, his brother had said. Sam respected and looked up to his older brother. Their mother had passed when they were little, so they lived with their father. But ever since then, Damien had been looking after himself and his little brother. Moving almost silently among the dead leaves and dry twigs, they made their way toward the edge of the woods. Damien's car was parked there. They didn't want to be late arriving at Chesterfield High school.

Chapter 2

The instant Sarah walked through the doors of Chesterfield high school, she was greeted by her two best friends. As soon as Cassie saw Sarah, she flung her arms around her and pulled her into a hug. Her long blonde hair touching Sarah's arms. We've missed you so much. Alex said as she embraced Sarah. Summer had ended and it was Fall, Sarah hadn't seen her friends since mid-June. As the group mingled some more with each other, the doors opened and two tall, dark and handsome figures emerged. Oh, my God, Cassie whispered. You can say that again, breathed Alex. From where she stood, Sarah could see that one had a lean, flat-muscled body. Faded jeans, a tight T-shirt, and a leather jacket. His hair was a brownish color. He wasn't tall, though. Just average height. The other figure, on the other hand, was a little taller. He too was wearing a leather jacket. Who are they? Alex asked. A long corridor stretched before them, as the two boys in jeans and leather jackets were disappearing through the office doorway up ahead. Cassie began to follow them, the other girls right behind her. Cassie slowed her pace as she walked up to the office, finally stopping and pretending to glance thoughtfully at the bulletin board by the door. There was a large window here, through which the entire office was visible. Cassie was trying to listen for the boys' names. Cassie, what are you doing? Sarah whispered, trying to call out to her. I'm trying to listen to their names. She murmured. Oh come on, Sarah grabbed her arm and led her away from the office window. After some time, the bell rang and the friends went their separate ways. Sarah walked down the corridor, up a flight of stairs, and into a classroom. She slid into an empty seat automatically and fixed her eyes on the teacher. Coincidentally, one of the boys she had just seen earlier, had walked into the classroom. He sat down at an empty seat next to Sarah. She snuck a small glimpse of him as she met his gaze. He was staring directly at her as he shot her a genuine smile. Sarah smiled back, before turning away slowly. She soon learned his name. After an hour, the bell rang and everyone flooded out of the classroom. The school day was going by fast and it was already lunch. Cassie was waiting for her near the cafeteria. She was outside, posed casually against a wall. She was talking to Alex as Sarah approached. Hi, ready to go in and eat? Sarah said briefly. The girls selected their lunch and went to find a place to sit. The boy we saw earlier this morning, his name is Sam Abbott. I sit next to him in math. Sarah briefed. Oooh, nice pedigree, am I right? Cassie said with a chuckle. What about the other guy? Alex said. Oh! He's in my biology class, and I sit right across from him. And his name is Damien, Damien Abbott. Cassie said. Are they brothers? Alex asked. They probably are. I mean, we did see them come in together. Sarah said, looking a little love-struck. Well, they're very mysterious, and I have my eye on one. Cassie said as she licked her lips. Wait, which one? Sarah asked with curiosity. Damien... Cassie said dreamily. Oh good, phew. Sarah said, relieved. Why? Wait, do you like Sam? Cassie said. Her blue eyes sparkled with excitement.

Uh, well he did smile at me in class, and I smiled back. Sarah said, blushing.

Sam was glad the school day was almost over. He wanted to get out of these crowded rooms and corridors, just for a few minutes. But he couldn't stop thinking about that girl he saw in class earlier in the day. Her soft mocha skin, her flowing, glossy, luxuriant hair, those captivating charcoal eyes. And that scent, that clean, crisp aroma. Like rose and lavender, and a tint of vanilla. Sam loved that smell, the second he walked through those doors of the school, he could smell it. And he desperately wanted to find out who's scent it was, and he finally did when he sat down next to that girl. "Sam! "Sam" Sam snapped out of his trance as Damien called his name repeatedly.

Chapter 3

The first light of dusk was streaking the night sky with a gloomy, murkiness purplish pink. Howls could be heard as Damien and Sam made their way through the woods. Snapping twigs, crunching leaves and cracking undergrowth with each step. Bats could be seen swarming the sky, and an owl could be heard hooting in the distance. The woodland seemed ominously quiet. They paused, looking up at the familiar tall shadowed pines stretching up like arrows into the sky. They knew they had reached their destination. There, they would meet with the Alpha Hounds to discuss business and hold meetings. The Alpha Hounds were a pack of ten wolves that come together to hold meetings or to hang out. As Damien and Sam shifted into wolf form, Cobalt, their leader and best friend sat amongst them and began briefing the pack. I have called you all here tonight, because I have learned some troubling news. Hunter Haynes and his Shadow Hounds have returned. A few gasps could be heard from the wolves as Cobalt continued briefing them. It's not clear on how they found us, but what matters is that we try and stay clear from them. Hunter won't stop until he gets what he wants. Revenge. As long as we stick together and avoid them, we'll be fine. Meeting adjourned. Cobalt said as he ended the meeting. Damien was furious, he could'nt believe the Shadow Hounds were back. All they did was cause nothing but trouble to the Alpha's. Hunter had killed one of the Alpha members, and Cobalt had also killed one of the Shadow pack members. This escelated to rivalty, and Hunter wanted revenge. Hunter used to be an Alpha hound, but he got kicked out. He wanted to be the leader of the Alpha's, and he was so jealous of Cobalt that he attacked him in a rage, which got him kicked out. He made his own pack, and ever since then, Hunter has been trying to seek revenge.

School the next day was merely a convenient place for Damien and Sam to bump into the person they least expected to see. They were walking down the hallway with their two best friends, Cobalt and Toby. They were greeted by a low whistle and a blonde haired guy walked towards them. Well, well, well, if it is'int the Alpha Hounds. His voice was husky and modulated. Hunter! What the hell are you doing here? Damien snapped, trying not to cause any comotion. Well, my pack and I are back in town, and we've got some buisness to take care of. Hunter said, smirking. How'd you find us anyway? Cobalt asked. We tracked you guys down. We're wolves remember. We have a strong sense of smell. Hunter said, before turning and walking away. And at that same exact moment, Sam could smell that scent again. That crisp, lavender, rose, vanilla smell. He turned his head to see the same girl he had seen the day before. She was walking with two other girls. Her friends, he assumed. Sam had to talk to her, he just had to. He just did'nt know how and when.

Chapter 4

By the time Sarah reached her locker, her friends had left and she was alone. This was it. This was the moment Sam had been waiting for. It's now or never. He said to himself, as he closed his eyes and took a breath. Hey, Sarah is it? His voice was silvery and gentle. Sarah smiled as she gave a nod. And you are Sam? Sarah said, closing her locker. Right. So, I was wondering if you were doing anything tonight? Sam said as they began to walk. No, why? Sarah was confused, but also curious. Great, cause there's this place I wanna take you to. They have the best food and I'm pretty sure you're gonna like it, Sam went on. Then no. I'm not doing anything tonight. Sarah blissfully replied. I'll pick you up at eight, then. Sam said before they exchanged numbers and departed.

Later, Sarah had told her friends what had happened and invited them over to her house. She had asked them to babysit Zoey, while she went on her date. But when they reached her house after picking up Zoey that afternoon, a chill ran down Sarah's back. She was excited but at the same time, nervous. After making a snack for Zoey, Sarah and her friends went upstairs to her room to debate on what she was going to wear that evening. We have got to find you the perfect outfit! Cassie said excitedly, as they went through Sarah's closet. It wasn't long till they found something. Ooh! How about this? Alex clutched the red, dashing, elegant dress to her chest before holding it up to show the other girls. Wow, you should definitely wear this one. Cassie said, admiring the dress. Time passed in a blur, and in no time Sam was already standing on Sarah's porch. After her friends hugged, and wished her luck, Sarah had emerged from the front door and Sam couldn't believe his eyes. Wow, you look… beautiful. His eyes went up and down Sarah's body. He led her to Damien's car, and they drove to a restaurant. As soon as they got to the restaurant, they found a seat and started chatting. It wasn't long until they engaged on a full conversation. Tell me about your family. Any siblings? Sam was intrigued by her. Uh, my parents both died in an accident. So I stay with my little sister, Zoey. Sarah said sadly as she looked down. Oh, I'm sorry, I had no idea. Sam felt sorry for her, he had no idea why he asked that question. He was just curious. My mom died too. I live with my dad and my older brother now. Sam spoke slowly. There was a short pause before Sarah spoke. Damien? Your brother's name is Damien? Sam nodded. He cocked his head to the side as he checked Sarah out again. His eyes scanning her body before meeting her gaze. He licked his lips as he took her hands in his, and laced his fingers through hers. As they reached the front porch, Sam turned to Sarah and tucked the wisps of hair behind her ear. He clasped her face in his hands and gently touched his lips to hers. They were too busy kissing, that neither of them noticed that someone in a black car was watching them and had driven off from view.

Chapter 5

It was Monday, and the weekend had gone by in a blur. Damien and Sam were talking amongst each other when they were interrupted by a familiar face. Hello Damien, hello Sam. Sorry for the intrusion, but I just wanted to say, Sam, that girl I saw you with last night… she's something, isn't she? Hunter prompted in a sly and vile manner. You stay the hell away from Sarah! Sam retorted. Listen, Hunter! Damien said, pinning him against a wall. You better not mess with my pack, or with my brother's girlfriend. Cause if you do, there's going to be some serious repercussions! Damien had his hands on Hunter's shirt collar. Damien had let Hunter go, and as they turned to leave, they let out a series of growls while giving each other menacing looks. Sam listen to me, you have to keep Sarah safe. Make sure Hunter doesn't go anywhere near her. You have to be with her at all times. Damien said once they were out of sight from Hunter. Got it. Sam nodded before wandering off to find Sarah. Hunter was dangerous, and Sam was willing to protect Sarah. Even if that meant her finding out his secret.

Chapter 6

After school, Sam had shown up to Sarah's locker with a picnic basket in hand. So, you're up for a picnic with me this afternoon? Sam said, holding up the picnic basket. Sure. But I need to pick up my sister from school first. You don't mind if she joins us? Sarah was packing the last of her books into her bag. Uh, no. Off course, she can come. Sam grinned. The walk to Zoey's school was not long, it only took them fifteen minutes to get there. As Zoey walked down the stairs and towards the entrance, she saw an unfamiliar guy with her sister. Sarah, who's this? She asked. Her sweet eyes flickered in the sunlight as her adorable face now became a confused one. I'm Sam, and you must be Zoey. Sarah's told me a lot about you. Sam had crouched down to her height. It's good to finally meet you. He flashed her a smile as he held out his hand. Well… its good to finally meet you too. Zoey shook his hand with a smile. Aren't you adorable? Sam said, with a slight chuckle as he arose from crouching down.

Sam had taken them to the nice parts of the forest. There, they could be alone and have some privacy. The air was rich with the scent of winter jasmine and a soft breeze. A few maple and pine trees circled around them as cool restful shady wind with light filtering lazily through the tree tops that meet high overhead and shut out the direct sunlight. Beautiful floral flowers are abloom on some nearby bushes. The grass is lush with an emerald, shamrock color, and a lake is overlooking the picturesque. Sam would sometimes come there on his own to think and get some peace. They had set up a huge blanket and began taking out the food. There were cookies, sandwiches, and cake to eat, and to drink was wine and water. Who wants a peanut butter and jelly sandwich? Sam asked, holding out a sandwich he just placed on a paper plate. Can I have one please? Zoey excitedly and eagerly requested. Of course you can, Sam passed the plate to Zoey, before getting another for Sarah. It was peaceful and quiet while they ate, except for their voices engaging in a conversation. Sam and Sarah were feeding each other cake, while Zoey played for a couple of minutes before Sam joined her. They had found a little white rabbit near some bushes. Sam had picked it up and held it towards Zoey so that she could pet it. Hey, you know what you should do? I think you should keep it. What do you think? Sam suggested as he gave Zoey a little smirk. Good idea, I'm gonna go ask Sarah. Zoey smiled at him before skipping away. Sara thought hard before answering. She looked at her sister, then at Sam who was gently holding the rabbit to his chest. Then before answering she sighed. Okay, fine. We can keep it. Zoey threw her arms around her sister while thanking her. None of them had noticed that someone had been watching them. By the time the sun started to set, Zoey was asleep in Sam's arms as they walked down the street to Sarah's house. She had unlocked the front door while holding the rabbit, then had let Sam in who was carrying a sleeping Zoey. He went up to her room and placed her on the bed, making sure she was covered. Not only did he have his brother and his friends as a pack, but he also had

Sarah and Zoey. He thought of them as his pack, and he had to do everything he could to protect them from Hunter and his pack.

Chapter 7

As Sarah stepped into the dining room of Sam Abbott's house, she studied her surroundings. The house was huge with an ancient vibe, the table was long and wooden with food already arranged. She was greeted by a man roughly to be in his mid 40's. She held out her hand and smiled as she shook the man's hand. The man had introduced himself as Paul Abbott. Sarah turned to see Damien who was smiling and embraced her as he greeted her. Dinner will be ready soon. Paul disappeared into the kitchen. Sarah spotted a framed photo of a woman. Is this your mom? She's really pretty. Sarah picked up the photograph. Thanks. Sam smiled. They sat down at the table as a chandelier hung above them. They said grace and began to eat, passing various foods around. So Sarah, any plans for when you graduate? Paul had asked, while passing the lamb chops to her. She was only a sophomore, but she already had plans. She wanted to be a nurse, like her mom. It's been her dream job ever since she was a kid. So your mom was a nurse? What about your father? Paul asked as he gave a sympathetic nod. He was a detective at the Chesterfield police department. Sarah prompted. Oh. Well I'm sorry about your parents. Paul placed his fork on the plate. Thats ok. Sarah took a sip of her water. How are you coping with this Sarah? He asked. Fine actually. It's just me and my little sister so… She wiped her mouth with a napkin. You mean to tell me you're staying by yourself? He blinked at her, surprised. It's okay, we're actually doing just fine. Sarah said, biting her lip. Well, if you need anything at all don't hesitate. Paul gave a concerned smile. I will, thank you sir. Sarah said, looking down this time and playing with her hands before placing them on the table again. Sam placed his hand on Sarah's before intertwining his fingers with hers. When they had finished dinner, Sarah hugged and thanked Paul before leaving with Damien and Sam.

Chapter 8

Lately, Sarah has been feeling like someone has been following her. Then she would tell herself, there's nothing there, you're just being paranoid. One minute she's hearing footsteps, and the other is utterly quiet. She didn't know what to believe. She had picked Zoey up from school, and as soon as they got home they found someone waiting for them on the front porch. Hunter was standing next to the rabbit hutch that they had gotten for the white rabbit which they had named Thumper. Sarah, good to finally meet you. He said enthusiastically. Uh, who are you? Sarah asked. Nothing to your concern. I just wanted to stop by and say hi. Hunter's blonde hair shimering in the wind. If you don't leave now, I'll call the police. Sarah said, reaching for her phone. Don't bother. I was just on my way. And Sarah… Thanks for the snack. That rabbit of yours, really hit the spot. Hunter whispered into Sarah's ear before turning the street and disappearing. Sarah felt sick to her stomach. How can someone do that? How did he even manage to get into her house and cook the rabbit? All those thoughts raced through Sarah's mind as she phoned Sam. As soon as Damien and Sam got there, she had told them what had happened. Zoey had just learned that her rabbit was dead, and tears were running down her cheek as Sam held her and Sarah in his arms while they sat on the couch. There was still blood and fur on the porch near the hutch, and Damien offered to clean it up since Sarah was in a state of shock and terror. I can't believe he would do this! That's it, that's the last straw. I've had it with this guy. The next time he goes near Sarah and Zoey, he's dead! Damien angrily snarled.

Chapter 9

Zoey had been waiting a good twenty minutes for her sister to show, but she hadn't come to pick her up yet. Sarah's always on time, she's never late. And if she was going to be late, she would ask Cassie or Alex to pick her up and take her home. Out of the blue, a boy with blonde hair had shown up. He crouched down to Zoey's height and began talking to her. He assumed she already learned his name from Damien and Sam, so he lied and gave her a fake name. Hi, I'm Brad. I'm Sarah's friend. Your sister's still busy at school, so she asked me to pick you up. Hunter said, trying to sound as nice as he possibly can. Aren't you that boy who was at our house yesterday? Zoey had recognized him. Nah, that was my twin brother, Jeff. He's always getting into trouble. And I think he likes your sister. Probably why he was at your house. Hunter said, winking. Seeing the boy wink, made Zoey giggle. She took the boy's hand, and off they went. When Sarah made it to Zoey's school, she saw that it was quiet and not many kids were waiting. She couldn't see Zoey though. She always waited for her in front of the gate. Luckily Sam was with her, and he had a hunch about what had happened to Zoey. He called Damien and told him to meet them in the woods while he and Sarah raced there. When they got there, they saw a black wolf sprawled across the grass with his front paws on a little girl as she laid down screaming.

Let her go, Hunter! Damien barked when he arrived. Hunter? Sarah thought of the boy she had seen on her porch the other day. The boy Damien and Sam told her about. But they said nothing about wolves. Sam? what's going on? She asked, confused. I'll tell you later. He said, before transforming into a wolf. Damien had already transformed and was lashing out at Hunter. Hunter had left the girl lying on that spot as he fought Damien on a different spot. Zoey! Sarah ran to her with Sam right behind her. Sam transformed back into a human. Listen, we have to go. It's not safe here. He said reassuring her. Sarah, I'm scared. Zoey cried. Get away from us. Sarah yelled. I'm sorry about all of this, but you are going to have to trust me. He begged. She looked at him, unsure then picked up Zoey. I'm taking you guys to Damien's car, you'll be safe there. Sam told Sarah as they began to walk. Meanwhile, Damien had pounced on Hunter and scratched him on his face, but too strong. He managed to push Damien off and scratch him and grasp him by the neck. He tugged and pulled by Damien's scruffy neck. Damien gave a small whine as blood started to flow. Suddenly, Sam rushed out from the trees and pounced on Hunter. His sharp teeth penetrating his leg. He had finally let go of Damien's neck and had managed to push Sam off. This isn't over! Hunter resorted as he ran off into the woods. When they got to Sarah's house, she had cleaned and rubbed ointment on Damien's scar and wounds. Then they had told Sarah and Zoey their secret. Damien and Sam had told them that they were wolves. Sarah couldn't believe her ears, she couldn't believe that werewolves actually existed. Zoey on the other hand was intrigued. She thought it was cool.

Ever since she found out about her boyfriend and his brother being wolves, Sarah initially told her friends about it. Wait, like wolves, wolves? Like Twilight? Alex queried as the four of them walked to Sarah's house. Sarah shrugged. Yeah, something like that I guess. Omg, so you and Sam are like the real-life versions of Bella and Jacob. Cassie stated. Uh... I wouldn't put it like that. Sarah doubted. Who are Bella and Jacob? Zoey asked when they reached the front door. Nobody Sarah replied, trying to avoid answering the question. I still think its awesome that you're dating a wolf. It only happens in fairytales but here you are dating a real one. Cassie plopped down on the couch as soon as they entered the house. I know. I guess it is pretty cool. Sarah placed her bag on the floor before making her way into the kitchen. Zoey, what do you think of Sam and Damien being wolves? Alex questioned. I think it's cool. Zoey sat down next to her. But remember, you can't tell anyone that they're wolves. Sarah called out from the kitchen. I know, I can keep a secret. Zoey smiled.

Chapter 10

As the days went by, Sarah had gotten used to Damien and Sam being wolves. It was winter break and Christmas had arrived. After spending some time with their father, Damien and Sam had gone over to Sarah's house to spend the holiday with them. They were chatting and drinking hot chocolate while Zoey played with her presents. Sarah didn't get her much, seeing that they didn't have a lot of money. Sarah had a job as a waitress at a local diner, which was a walking distance to her house. Sam had a little box wrapped in paper. He smiled as he gave it to Sarah. Sarah smiled as she took it from him and unwrapped the paper before opening it. Her heart skipped a beat as she saw what was inside. It was a beautiful silver necklace with a ruby stone that hung down. Thank you, it's beautiful. She replied as Sam helped her put it on. Damien and Sam were whispering among each other. That reminds me, there's still one last present we have for you guys. It's in the car, we just have to go and get it. Damien said as him and Sam got up from the couch and walked towards the door. A few minutes later they emerged through the door. Sam was carrying plastic bags from a store, as Damien followed carrying a Siberian Husky puppy. It was white and a grey color. Sarah and Zoey were surprised, they both had their hands to their mouths. After Hunter ate your rabbit, we were devastated, and we decided to get you guys another pet. Only this time, something Hunter can't eat. Sam explained as Damien placed the tiny pup on Sarah's lap. And seeing how you guys like wolves, It's a wolfdog. Uh, not necessarily. It's a husky but it's like a wolfdog. They howl like wolves. Damien added. Oh my gosh. I don't know what to say. Thank you guys so much. Sarah said as she got up and hugged the two boys. As they embraced, Zoey had joined them making it a group hug.

Chapter 11

Damien and Sam were always around. They were always by Sarah and Zoey's side. It was still winter break, three days after Christmas. The sky was overcast with clouds and chilly winds were blowing. Zoey was playing in the snow with her new puppy which they had named Max. She was with Damien, who was throwing snowballs at her and pushing her down a hill on a sled. Meanwhile, Sam had taken Sarah ice skating on a frozen lake not far from where Damien and Zoey were. The ice was smooth for skating on, and Sarah had held on to Sam. She wasn't a good skater, she was a bit wobbly but soon she was getting used to it. They were holding hands and gliding nicely on the ice, when Sarah lost her balance and toppled over, falling back right into Sam's arms. For a moment they gazed into each other's eyes, not paying attention to what was going on around them. Then unexpectedly, Sam planted a kiss on her lips. They giggled as he helped her stand upright. They then spotted Damien who was holding Zoey in one hand, and Max's leash in the other. He motioned for them to come. They went back to Sarah's house to have some cookies and hot chocolate. Eventually, after the hot chocolate, Sarah had fallen asleep on Sam's lap. He looked at her before planting a kiss on her cheek and covering her with a blanket. Damien had done the same for Zoey as the two brothers continued to watch TV.

Chapter 12

Damien and Sam Abbott had been called into their father's office for unknown reasons. They had done nothing wrong, so they thought it was for some family meeting about the Shadow Hounds since they've always been called in for that purpose. Paul Abbot had been trying to stop the Shadow Hounds for many months now, especially Hunter's father. Joseph Haynes. He and Joseph were moral enemies that hated one another all because they never saw eye to eye when they used to be in the same pack. Paul wanted equality and high standards for their pack. He wanted what was best for their pack, but Joseph disagreed. Joseph wanted complete control and power. He wanted the wolves to train for a battle that never came. Ever since Damien and Sam told them that the Shadow Hounds were back, he wanted to stop them once and for all.

I called you both in here because there's something I've been wanting to discuss with you two. Paul said. What is it, dad? Damien asked. It's about your friend, Sara. Paul got up from his office chair and walked toward his sons. What about her? The boys looked at each other. I've just been thinking about her current situation. Paul began. I gave a little bit of thought, and what if she stayed here with us? He looked at his sons for clarification. Uh, why would she do that? Damien had a look of confusion. Because she's only a child living on her own raising her sister. Which doesn't seem right to me. Dad, she's only seventeen. Sam. My point exactly. She's far too young to be living alone and raising a little girl on her own. And what does she do for financial circumstances? Paul walked over to the small whiskey bar and poured himself a glass of whiskey. Well, she told me she does have a job as a waitress at a diner. Sam exclaimed. That's not enough to support her. Besides, she needs to be safe from Hunter and his pack. Paul pointed out. Damien and Sam never thought of it that way. I guess you're right. Damien rubbed his chin with his fingers. Fine, okay. We'll help her move in tomorrow. Sam crossed his arms. Excellent! I will be awaiting her arrival Paul gulped down the remaining substance left in his whiskey glass

Chapter 13

Sarah removed all her clothes from the closet and placed them on the bed, beside two large suitcases. Cassie and Alex had gone over to help. You know, you could always stay with me. That is if you don't mind having two young toddlers constantly running around and making a lot of noise. Alex offered. Alex, I don't think Sarah could handle your little brothers. Cassie replied while folding a shirt before placing it into one of the suitcases. Guys its ok, Zoey and I will be just fine with Damien and Sam. Sarah assured them. But if you have a problem you know you can just call us,right? Alex, I'm not leaving town, its just a couple of blocks away. Besides, we'll still see each other at school. Sarah chuckled. Yeah, you've got to stop worrying. Cassie placed a couple of Sarah's shoes in some shoe boxes.

Alright, Zoey's all packed and ready to go. Sam and Damien came into the room with Zoey's suitcases. Zoey trailed behind them holding a cardboard box. Zoey. what is that? Sarah questioned when she saw the box. My stuffed animals. Zoey loved her toys, especially her stuffed animals. They were a constant reminder of her parents seeing as when they were still alive, they woud always buy her some so that she could add to her collection. You got your shoes, dresses, tops, toothbrush? Sara queried while trying to zip up her suit case. Yeah, we've got everyhing.

We've even packed for Max. Sam responded, clipping on Max's leash. Well... I guess that's everything. Sarah went into the bathroom to pack her remaining stuff while Damien and Sam helped load the bags into the car. Sara took one last look at the house before joining everyone outside. She handed the keys to the new home owners before placing a sold sign on the front lawn. She pulled Cassie and Alex in for a group hug and embraced for a good ten minutes before Zoey joined in. The two friends leaned up against Cassie's car as they watched Damien's car pull away from the driveway before disappearing into the street.

It only took them thirty minutes to get to the Abbot house. Damien had opened the door for them as Sarah and Zoey step into the house with Max on a leash. They take in their surroundings just as Paul arrives to greet them. Sarah, how nice to see you again. He embraced her before fixing his eyes on Zoey. And you must be Zoey. I'm Paul. Damien and Sam's father. He introduced as he shook the little girl's hand. Hi. She said shyly. Thanks again for letting us stay here, Mr Abbot. Sarah smiled while expressing her gratitude. But of course, this is your new home now. And please call me Paul. Boys, please show Sarah and Zoey to their rooms. Paul instructed. Damien and Sam took their suitcases before escorting them up the staircase and down the hall to some guest bedooms. Sarah, this will be your room. Damien opened the door to a cosy looking room with a queen sized bed that consist of a wooden headboard. The room also featured some rustic looking furniture, including two bed side tables, a large wooden wardrobe, an antique dressing table with a mirror, some drawers and a large window over looking the garden.

This is beautiful. Sarah said while admiring her new room. We're glad you like it. Now Zoey, are you ready to see your room? Sam turned to her. Yeah, Iets go see mine. She replied excitedly. The second room had more of a victorian vibe to it. It consisted of another queen sized bed, an antique wardrobe, dressing table and another large window. Wow Zoey, what do you think? Sarah asked while looking around. I love it. She placed her box of stuffed animals on the floor and began to open it. Max can sleep here with me, right? Zoey placed her stuffed animals on the bed. Yeah, of course. Her sister nodded in response. We're glad you guys like your rooms. Damien said, watching Zoey who was aleady feeling like she was home. Thank you guys so much. I really appreciate it. Sarah wrapped her arms around the two boys.

That night, they had a casual dinner before Sarah helped Zoey get ready for bed. Don't worry, you'll be fine. Sarah sat next to her on the edge of the bed. I'm right next door if you need me. And remember, Max is gonna be right here with you. She brushed her sister's hair with her hand. I love you. Zoey murmured while holding her teddy bear. I love you too. Sarah planted a kiss on her forehead before getting up and making her way towards the door. She looked back at her sister before opening the door and leaving.

Chapter 14

Ever since they moved into the Abbot house, Sarah and Zoey have obliged to the rules and respected Paul's boundarries. Now and then they would also pitch in and help with the chores. Sarah and Zoey loved staying with the Abbots. They were like the family they never had, seeing as they lost theirs. Sarah never considered replacing her real family with the Abbots. She still loved them and kept them close to her heart. But the Abbots were like a second family to her and her sister. They would do family things together, like have family game nights, watch movies and have barbeques in the backyard. The backyard was huge with a lot of space for Zoey and Max to run around and play. There was even a pool which Zoey loved. It was a sunny Saturday afternoon, and everyone was down at the pool enjoying themselves. Paul was at the outdoor kitchen, mending the meat on the grill while the kids splashed around in the pool. Sam and Damien were playing with Zoey in the pool while Sarah watched from one of the pool chairs. Come on in Sarah, the water's great. Damien insisted with Zoey on his shoulders. Yeah, and we're having a lot of fun in here. We're just missing one more person. Sam coaxed while pretending to look around. Okay, I'm coming. Sarah got up from her chair before making her way into the pool. As soon as she got into the pool, Sam pulled her close and kissed her. But before he could place her onto his shoulders, her phone rang. I'm sorry, just give me one second. Sarah got out of the pool to answer it. She assumed it was Alex and Cassie seeing as she invited them over. As soon as she reached the front door, she flung her arms around them. Woah, this place is huge. Alex commented as they walked in. Just wait until you see the backyard. Sarah led them back to the pool. Cassie! Alex! Welcome! Paul greeted when he saw them. Thanks again Paul for letting me bring my friends over. Sarah beamed. Of course, the more the merrier. Mi casa es su casa. He laughed. Alex, Cassie! Zoey ran over to them when she saw them. They greeted her before greeting the boys who were still in the pool. As soon as the girls got into the pool, Sam had lifted Sarah on to his shoulders just as Damien did the same with Cassie.

Paul was grinning from ear to ear as he watched everyone having fun in the pool. There's nothing that Paul wants more than for his sons to be happy. The death of their mother had really effected them and put a strain on their lives, but ever since they met Sarah and Zoey it was like a weight had been lifed off their shoulders. They made them feel whole again, and they're the ones that brought back their smiles. The same smile they had back when they were only five years old before their mother had passed. Sarah, Zoey, Alex and Cassie are the ones that helped them move on and get their lives back on tack. And he was eternally grateful. The outside patio table had been set and lunch was soon served as everyone gathered aound the table. Now, I want to take the time to make a toast and say thank you all for being here on this wonderful afternoon. But more inportantly, I want to thank Sarah and Zoey. Ever since you came into my son's lives, you've changed it for the better. After losing the boy's mother, there had been some heartache in the family and we were never the same after that. But when I saw the way you and your sister made Sam and Damien smile and laugh today, I was just so joyus. So thank you. Paul looked over at Cassie and Alex. And thank you both as well for being good friends to the boys. To family and to new friendships. He raised his glass as they all clinked them.

When lunch ended, the girls cleared the table and washed all the dishes while the boys tidied up the barbeque area. So, how are things going with you and Sam? Cassie asked while she dried the dishes before handing them to Alex to put away. Everything is great. Why? Sara queried handing a wet plate to Cassie. Oh, no reason. Its just you two were getting really clingy at the table. Cassie pointed out. Sarah looked at her. So? So? You guys could'nt keep your hands off each other. Wait a minute... Cassie's eyes widened. Did you guys.... Cassie! Of course not! Oh my Goodness. Sarah covered her mouth with her hand as the girls started giggling. What's going on in here? Damien asked when he and Sam heard the giggles. Oh nothing. Cassie lied. Come on, we heard you guys giggling. Ok fine. We were just talking about Cassie's crush. That's all. Alex blurted out something. And whom may this be? Damien questioned. Uh... some guy who goes to our school. His name starts with a D, I think. Alex continued to lie. Oh really? And does this guy have a brother? He continued to inquire. Yes, he does. Alex nodded. Alex! Cassie signaled her to stop. Damien looked over at Cassie. Well, I feel the same way. He smirked, making her blush. When the boys were out of view, Cassie gave Alex a playful shove. Why did you do that? What, I sorta panicked. Sorry. But look on the bright side, Damien likes you. Alex responded. He does, does'nt he? Cassie licked her lips. You guys are so lucky. You both have werewolves crushing over you. Alex sighed. Don't worry, it will happen to you too. Sarah assured her. Yeah, I bet there's a hot werewolf waiting for you somewhere. You'll see. Cassie placed her hand on her shoulder. Alex nodded. Someday.

Chapter 15

A year has gone by with no trace of Hunter and his pack. Zoey was already in the third gade, and Max their Siberian Husky pup has grown into a large, beautiful dog. Damien and Sam have been suspicious and weary of Hunter. There's no news about Hunter's whereabouts. Cobalt, one of Sam and Damien's friends had informed them. Just to be safe, we need to be on high alert. We'll never know when Hunter and his pack will strike. Damien sniffed the air around him, but could'nt pick up Hunter's scent. Got it. I'll let the others know. Cobalt said as he closed his locker. Sam and I were going to go out tonight, but we were thinking of making it a double if you're interested. Sarah offered as the girls walked over to Cassie's locker. What about Alex? She asked. I'm babysitting Zoey with Mr Abbot, i guess. She replied. Then sure, I'm down for a double date. Cassie grinned. Great, I'll text Sam and let him know the details. Sarah took out her phone from her pocket. Damien and Cassie had been dating ever since the barbeque. After the girls informed Damien about Cassie's crush, he had returned and asked her for her number. Alex, are you sure you don't want to come? They asked her again. I told you, I'll be fine. You guys go and have fun. She urged them. The final bell rang as kids dispersed from the school.

Joeseph Haynes sat in his black Lincoln as he watched his

son decsend the steps before making his way to the car. How was school? He turned to face him after getting in. Fine. Why? Hunter looked at him bewildred. We need to talk. Joseph pulled out of the school before driving off. About what? Hunter queried. The future of the Shadow Hounds. Joeseph kept his eyes glued to the road. His shades glistening in the sunlight. When they arrived back at their manor, Joseph led his son to his office before pouring himself some whisky. Sit son, sit. He motioned to the chairs at his desk. Hunter shrugged as he took a seat. I think we're ready for our plan to come at view. Don't you think son? He removed his shades and placed them on the table. Finally. You want me to go and tell the rest of the Pack? He asked, slightly getting up. Not yet. You see, those stupid Alpha Hounds think we're MIA (missing in action) and they're probably not worrying about us anymore. Its all just a damn trick from us truly. Its all part of the plan. He explained. So when are we going to attack? Hunter asked. All in due time son. There's no rush. But there is one problem... The girl. What about her? Hunter sat up in his chair. We need to somewhow get rid of her. Once we try to separate Damien and Sam from her, it will probably be easier to take her down. But for now, just keep an eye on them. Just watch their every move until the Shadow Hounds are ready to strike. Joseph took another sip of his whisky.

Sarah and Cassie were at the Abbot house getting ready for their double date. Why can't I come again? Zoey was sitting on Sarah's bed, fidgeting with her teddy bear. I've already told you, its a date. Sarah replied while applying her make up in the mirror. Unless you have a boyfriend, then you could probably come with us. Do you have a boyfriend? Cassie asked. Zoey nodded, No. I think I'm too young to have a boyfriend. Yes you are. And don't worry, you'll stay here with Mr Abbot and Alex. I know you and Alex will probably have some fun together. Sarah smiled. Girls, you ready? Damien called out from the bottom of the staircase. Yeah, just a sec. Sarah and Cassie checked themselves in the mirror before leaving the room. Alright dad we're leaving. Damien grabbed the keys from the counter. Paul stood in the doorway of his office. Ok, you guys enjoy yourselves. Have fun. Alex added as she placed her hands on Zoey's shoulders. The two couples went to a local Bowling alley and upon arriving and getting their shoes, Sam had led Sarah to one of the booths where he helps her with her shoes. Aww, you are such a gentleman. Thank you. She says when he is done. You welcome. He smiles and looks up at her. So, what's it going to be? Damien asked as he tapped the screen. How about we do a boys versus girls game? Cassie suggested with a smirk. You're on. Just know, you girls are going down. Damien said when he was finished setting up the score board. Cassie was the first to go. She picked up a bowling ball and positioned herself on the lane before making her move. The ball whisked down the lane knocking them all over. Yes! That's a strike for the girls. Beat that boys. Cassie exulted while moving a strand of blonde hair from her face. Don't think we won't. Sam got up and chose a ball from the rack. After rolling it, he watched as it sped down the lane before making it another strike. He high fived his brother as Sarah got up to get her ball. Unfortunetly, she only managed to knock down three pins. Hey, its ok. You did allright. Next time you just have to keep your back staight, and when you roll the ball you bring your arm back like this before jolting it forward. Sam held out Sarah's arms as she held out the bowling ball while standing behind her and instructing her. Is'nt that considered cheating? Cassie teased while watching Sam and Sarah. No, I'm just helping her and showing her what do do. Sam responded as Damien took his turn.

The game continued on for about an hour before finishing with the girls winning. Afterwards, they drove to a resturant to have dinner where they spent the remainder of the night. When they arrived back at the Abbot house, Cassie and Alex left together in Cassie's car. Sarah opened her sister's bedroom door, to find her fast asleep. She smiled at the outcome before closing the door and going to her room. After changing into her nightdress and removing her make up, Sarah had sat down at the dressing table and began brushing her hair before hearing a knock at the door. As soon as she opened it, Sam crashed his lips to hers as he made his way into the room. He lunged at her, pushing her against the wall and pinning her. she responded passionately, returning his kiss eagerly. She moans into his mouth as his hands trail alongside her contrast lace nightdress. Sam starts biting and kissing the side of her neck as he fidgets with one of her straps and pulls it down. He then proceeds to lift her nightdress up and remove it, revealing her lingerie. Sam takes a moment to admire her body, smirking as his eyes wander. He picks her up and in response she wraps her legs around his waist. He places her on the bed and takes off his shirt before hovering over her. His inner wolf getting ready to come out and play. He gave her a trail of kisses from her neck to her stomach before taking thngs a little bit more further.

Chapter 16

The following morning, Sarah had her head on Sam's bare chest as they laid in bed together. I can't believe we just did that. Sarah breathed. She has never done anything like that before. She was only Seventeen, too young to be sleeping around with boys. But she has no idea what came over her last night. Maybe it was the fact that she felt his erection behind her when he was showing her how to bowl or how clingy they were being on the day of the barbeque. Either way, they felt like they were ready. Sarah was feeling good inside. She did'nt know what it was, but it was rather sensational. Sam kissed her on the forehead. I'm just glad you liked it. What's not to like? She asked while looking up at him. Just the fact that I could;ve given you wolf babies if we had'nt used protection. Wolf babies? Is that even possible with a human and a wolf? She queried. No, you have to be a wolf in order to conceive wolf babies. In this case, wolf cubs. He answered. What's it like being a wolf? She questioned. Well...Its kinda like being an animal I guess. You know, hunting for food, howling at the moon. But we also have these pack meetings in the forest. Sam explained while caressing her arm. Wait, so do you actually eat uncooked animals? Sarah cringed as she sat up. In our wolf forms, yes. But not as humans. Oh thank goodness, she laid back down next to him, relieved. He gave a slight chuckle. Don't worry, being a wolf is'nt as bad as it seems.

It has its flaws but you get use to it.
Have you always been a wolf? What's with all the questions? He interjected. Sorry, I'm just really curious. She replied. He smiled and shook his head. No, not always. It started after my mother died. Sam? What happened? Why are you and Damien wolves? You've never told me. She murmured. Sam sighed before restating his story. We were in Whitebridge where I'm originally from. My dad, Damien and my self were walking home one night when we saw the Moon's Crescent. We also noticed Hunter standing on a hill with his father and the Shadow Hounds. So we decided to investigate and see what was going on. Eventually, they were all absorbing the power of the moon's Crescent which granted them the power to shapeshift into wolves. Soon, we had also absorbed the moon's power. Sarah was just about to ask about the Moon's Crescent when they heard a voice calling Sam. Duty calls. He said getting out of bed and putting on his shirt. I guess I'll see you later. He kissed her before leaving.
Sarah found herself in the libary of the Abbot home, looking for any books that could tell her about the Moon's Crescent. Ever since Sam told her about it she had been intrigued and wanted to know more about it. She skimmed through the shelves, but all she could find were old books of folk tale and literature. Paul poked his head through the libary door and saw Sarah struggling. Can I help you find anything? He asked. I'm just looking for a book on the Moon's Crescent. Paul looked at her. The Moon's Crescent? Yeah, Sam told me about it and I'm really intrigued to find out more about it. She placed another book back on the shelf. Paul rubbed his chin with his thumb as he pondered. Here, I think I might have

something. He left the libary and went to his office to retrieve a book from his shelf. Here, I hope this helps. He handed her the book. The wolve's of Whitebridge. She read the tiltle as her hand caressed the cover. The book looked like an ancient journal, and had a brown cover. She thanked him before leaving for work.

It says here that the moon's Crescent is an urban legend in the town of Whitebridge. Alex read what was in the book. The three friends were sitting at a booth in the diner. That's where Sam and Damien are from. Sarah said. According to this book, The Moon's Crescent only happens once every 5 years. A full moon appears aluminating the sky in a blue sapphire color as it glows and shines. It draws townspeople to it, and once they're close enough, it transforms them into wolves. Alex continued to read on. Woah... They looked at each other. This is all so mysterious. I like it. Cassie smirked and creepy. Like who wants a blue moon hovering over the sky and turning people into wolves? Alex added as she closed the book. Kind of, but its also fascinating at the same time. Sarah placed her hands on the cover. Speaking of which, Sarah you are glowing. Right Alex? Cassie remarked before turning to her. Yeah, Cassie's right. You've never actually glowed like this before. Which could only mean one thing. You and Sam did it. Cassie said. What??? Oh come on don't try to deny it. We won't judge you. Alex said. Sarah sighed, Fine. We did. Cassie and Alex screeched. Oooh, Sarah Cooper lost her virginity to a werewolf. Cassie teased. I did and I admit, it felt pretty good. Sarah blushed. Sarah, get back to work! There's tables that need serving over here. Her boss called out from behind the front counter. Oop, I gotta get back to work. She said getting up from her seat just as Damien and Sam arrived with Zoey. Hey guys. How was the park? She greeted them before kissing her boyfriend. It was great. Zoey replied as she slid inside the booth next to Alex. Alight, I gotta run. She said as she left in a hurry.

Chapter 17

A few days later Hunter walked into Chesterfield diner, he spotted Sarah standing at the front counter. He let out a mischievous smile before wandering over to her. Sarah, long time no see. He greeted her. Hunter? She replied, surprised to see him. W-w-what are you doing here? She stammered. Oh I just came to see you one last time before I leave. He said, folding his arms. Oh Y-youre leaving? Why is that? She sounded nervous. Yeah, my dad and I just have some things we have to take care of back in Whitebridge. What's the matter Sarah? You seem nervous. He asked, sensing her demeanour. No, I'm-I'm fine. She replied. I'm a wolf Sarah, I can sense the fear inside you. You don't have to be scared of me. I'm not going to hurt you. Yet. That last word sent chills down her spine. I should go. Bye Sarah. His voice was intimidating. Her heart was pounding in her chest as she quickly grabbed her phone from the back and dialed Sam's number. After a ten minute wait, Sam and Damien finally arrived with the girls. Luckily, they had all been hanging out together when she called. Oh my God Sarah, are you okay? Cassie and Alex embraced her. Yeah, I'm fine, just a little panicky. She led them to a booth while draping an arm around Zoey. Yeah, you sounded scared on the phone. Sam kissed and hugged her before taking a seat. I can't believe Hunter just showed up out of the blue like that. Damien fumed. Is Sarah going to be ok? Zoey asked. She's going to be fine honey. Don't worry. Cassie tried reassuring her. "I'm not going to hurt you yet?" What does that even mean? Alex asked as she restated Hunter's words. Hunter's up to something. Him and his dad are planning something. Sam responded. Yeah, but what? Cassie said. He told me he and his dad were leaving to go back to Whitebridge. Sarah recalled. What? When? Damien queired. I don't know, he just said he had some things he had to take care of over there. The Moon's Crescent. Damien and Sam both said as they looked at each other.

Chapter 18

The night sky is changing overhead with a patchy sky and stars seen in glimpses through tree breaks. Dark tree trunks cast shadows and clumps of bushes are seen in the distance. Barely visible black trails snaking through the undergrowth as the moon shines through a lattice of leaves, giving light to the forest. The only sounds that could be heard is an owl resting on a tree branch and twigs and leaves crunching as paws maneuvered through the area. Damien sniffed the air for some time before turning around to face Hunter. What do you want Damien? Whatever it is, make it quick. I have some things I need to attend to. Hunter's black fur almost camouflaged in the darkness. Sarah told me you showed up at the diner to see her. She told us what you said. Damien said as Sam emerged in his brown wolf form. I knew that girl would squeal. Hunter sneered. You stay the hell away from Sarah! Sam snarled, showing his teeth. Please, you two don't scare me one bit. Hunter rolled his eyes. Ditto. Damien replied. Well, you should be scared. You and your pack. Cause you have no idea what I'm capable of and what my plan is. Hunter insinuated. We know exactly what you're planning. The moon's Crescent. You want to go back to Whitebridge and absorb the power again so that you can be even more powerful and turn into a Rahu wolf. Damien disclosed. Very good. I did'nt think you guys were that smart. But there's no stopping me this time. As Hunter turned around to leave, Sam pounced in front of him to block his path. You want to fight? Fine, let's fight. Hunter growled as he lashed out and scratched Sam on the cheek, making him fall to the ground. He hovered over him and pressed his two front paws down on his throat. Let him go Hunter. Damien pounced on him, pinning him to the ground. Suddenly, Hunter's Shadow pack appeared from the depths of the forest and surrounded them. Look at that, six against two. What's it going to be Alphas? He looked at them in a cunning manor while Damien still had him pinned down. Damien slowly backed away from him. We're not going to let you do this, Hunter. We'll stop you one way or another. Sam and Damien glared at him before disappearing through the woods.

Chapter 19

Sarah was cleaning Sam's wound on his cheek while he and Damien retold the story of Hunter's plan to Sarah and their father. So Joseph and Hunter plan on using the moon's Crescent to evolve into Rahu's and take over wolf kind, which I presume. We have to stop them, we can't let them do that. Paul responded. Wait, what is a Rahu and I thought you said the Moon's Crescent made people into wolves? Sarah looked at Sam. Rahu is a type of wolf form in wolf evolution. It is one of the most powerful wolf forms in history. The Moon's Crescent can transform humans into wolves, but while the human is still a wolf, it can also evolve them into Rahus, Paul explained. Will Damien and Sam evolve into a Rahu? She asked. No, only the Moon's Crescent has the power to evolve a wolf into a Rahu. He turned to Damien and Sam, the Moon's Crescent will appear three nights from now in Whitebridge. I suggest we pack and leave. When are we leaving? Damien questioned. Tomorrow morning. What about Sarah and Zoey? Sam asked. Oh, they're coming with us. We can't just leave them here by themselves. Paul said as he disappeared into his office. We're going to Whitebridge? I get to see where you guys grew up. She smiled. Zoey, guess what? She called her sister over who was busy watching TV in the living room. What? She walked over to them with Max. You, me, Sam, Damien, and Mr. Abbot are going on a little trip together. Like on vacation? Sorta, but it's more of a business trip.

You remember the plan right? Joseph asked his son as they sat in his car. Yes, dad, I know what to do. Hunter replied. Good. Now let's get this plan into action. Wolves were howling in the forest as it could be heard from the Abbot house and Damien and Sam knew exactly what it was. That's Cobalt. He's calling us. Damien used his sharp wolf hearing ability. Sarah, you and Zoey have to stay here with my dad. Hunter could be looking for us, and you guys are safer here. Sam kissed her before leaving with Damien. As soon as they stepped outside, they transformed into wolves before making their way to the forest. Nice to see you again Cobalt. Tony, one of the Shadow Hounds sneered. Cobalt snarled before pouncing on him as a fight erupted between the two packs. Not long after, Damien and Sam had arrived. Winston, what's going on? They asked one of their other pack members. Hunter and the shadow Hounds have started a brawl. Winston informed before attacking another wolf. Sarah and Zoey were watching a movie on the couch when they heard the doorbell ring. They looked at each other as they got up to answer it. They slowly made their way to the door and opened it to find Joseph and Hunter standing outside. Sarah quickly tried closing the door, but Joseph had his foot in the way. They burst through the door as they let themselves in. Paul! Sarah called out as she held Zoey close to her. What's going on? He said as he stepped out of his office to find Joseph and Hunter in his house. Hello Paul. Joseph greeted him cunningly. What the hell do you think you're doing here? Paul spat. To get what we wanted. Revenge. Joseph glared at him. Take Zoey, and go and hide. Paul murmured into Sarah's ear. She nodded in response before picking up Zoey and running to the staircase. Get her. Joseph instructed his son to follow her.

Joseph pulled out a pistol handgun and pointed it at Paul. Listen, Joseph, you don't have to do this. He put his hands up. Oh, but I do. His hand was now on the trigger. Look, we can settle this as wolves, fight our way to the death. Paul suggested. Fine. Joseph placed his gun on a table and transformed into a vigorous black wolf. After Paul transformed, they pounced on each other. Meanwhile, when Sarah reached the top of the staircase, she had put Zoey down and told her to run and hide. What about you? Aren't you going to hide too? She asked. I will, I just need to talk to Hunter. Maybe I can reason with him or something. She hugged her sister and watched her run off and disappear into one of the rooms. Oh, Sarah... Hunter called as he climbed up the stairs. He gave her an evil grin when he saw her at the top of the stairs. Damien and Sam were still in the forest fighting the Shadow Hounds when they realized Hunter was nowhere to be found. Wait a minute, where's Hunter? But the Shadow Hounds just kept quiet and let them ponder. Sarah! They looked at each other and realized that her life was in danger. P-please Hunter, you don't have to do this. Let's just talk about this, ok? Sarah shivered as he crept closer. There's nothing to talk about. He made his hand into a fist. Sarah had turned around and was just about to make a beeline for the hallway, but before she could even take off running, Hunter grabbed her arm and pulled her towards him. He pushed her onto the ground and pounced on her while transforming into a wolf and trying to attack her. Sarah tried her best to push him off and hold him back, but she was weak and helpless underneath the strong wolf. Sarah! Sam and Damien called out from the foyer as they arrived back at the house. Help! She screamed in agony as the two boys made their way up the stairs to see the horrifying sight of Hunter who was on top of Sarah. Get the hell off of her! Sam transformed and lunged at him, pushing him off of Sarah. Sarah, are you ok? Damien asked as he aided her. Sarah! Zoey cried out as she scampered out from one of the rooms and into her sister's arms. Zoey, I told you to go and hide. She fretted. I did, but I heard you scream and I was scared. She replied. Meanwhile, Paul and Joseph were still going at it with each other. Paul had managed to fling Joseph off of him and send him flying across the floor. He looked at the gun which was sitting on the table next to him and in a fit of fear he turned back into a human and grabbed the gun. He pointed it at Joseph. What? What are you going to do? Shoot me? Go ahead. But you don't have the guts to do it. He provoked. Screw you, Joseph. I've had just enough of you and your crap. For years my boys and I have been trying to stop you and your son, and end this war between the Shadows and the Alphas. And now I can finally put an end to it. Goodbye Joseph. He cocked the pistol and took aim. Joseph charged at him and when he was just about to strike, the gun went off. Dad!!! No!!! Hunter stopped fighting with Sam and rushed downstairs to find his dad. Joseph was lying on the floor and had turned back into a human as he bled from his wound. Dad, please be ok. Stay with me ok? Don't go. Hunter sobbed. Finish what we started and continue with the plan. I love you son. Joseph coughed and croaked before closing his eyes. Dad, Dad, No. I love you... Hunter sniffed. He looked up at Paul with the most threatening eyes you could ever imagine. You're dead! You hear me? You're a dead man Paul Abbot. I'm gonna kill all of you! He raged as he left the house. While Damien went to aid his father, Sarah and Zoey were crying into Sam's chest as he sat down on the floor next to them and comforted them as he brought them into a hug.

Chapter 20

The following morning everyone had gotten up bright and early to get ready for their trip to Whitebridge. Sarah laid in bed thinking about the events of last night. She had never gone through anything like that before, she was still feeling eerie, and let alone her sister who was only eight was still haunted by it. She looked at Zoey who was still asleep in the bed next to her, clutching a teddy bear to her chest. After what had happened last night, she was too scared to sleep in her room so Sarah let her climb into her bed. Sarah picked up her phone from the bedside table and checked the time which was only reading 8:30 am. She sent a quick text message to Cassie letting her know that they will probably be leaving at around tenish. She looked around the room and noticed some of her clothes scattered around on the dressing table bench. Ok, time to get to work. She said as she got out of bed and walked over to the wardrobe. She opened it and placed her two suitcases on the bed. Sarah? Zoey sat up in the bed. Hey Zo. She greeted her. What are you doing? She asked rubbing her eyes. I'm packing. We're going to Whitebridge today, remember? Oh yeah. She yawned. Why don't you go and take a bath while I start packing, ok? Sarah said. But I'm tired. Zoey replied groggily. You can sleep in the car, ok? She kissed her on the forehead. Ok. She said, getting out of bed. After Zoey left the room, Sarah turned her attention back on her suitcase. She first took out what she was going to wear before gathering and folding her clothes. She packed them neatly in both suitcases before zipping them up.

She took a quick shower and had thrown on some denim shorts, sneakers, a top, and a hoodie. After helping Zoey pack her things, they went downstairs for breakfast. Good morning girls. Paul greeted while frying some eggs. Morning. They greeted back. Damien and Sam were already seated at the kitchen table as the girls took a seat. How's she holding up? Damien asked, motioning to Zoey. She's fine. Still terrified about what happened last night, we're both are. Sarah replied. It will be ok. And we are so sorry about what happened. Damien apologized. It's not your fault. You guys didn't know Hunter and his father would be here. Sarah empathized. But we were not there to protect you. Sam added. The important thing is that we're all okay and that when we get to Whitebridge, we are going to take Hunter down. Sarah's right. It's time to end this wolf war once and for all. Hunter and His father have been problematic to us and to Whitebridge for over ten years now. Paul said as he placed a plate of pancakes on the table. Ten years? Sarah questioned. Yep. Hunter used to bully Sam and me when we were kids, then as he got older he learned about the moon's Crescent and its power. And ever since he turned into a wolf, his being causing chaos and havoc in Whitebridge. Damien explained. Like what? Sarah plopped a piece of her pancake in her mouth. Things like stealing meat from the butcher, attacking people for no apparent reason. People were scared of him and his Shadow Hounds. Damien replied. He's a menace to Whitebridge, and he needs to be stopped. Paul added.

After breakfast, Paul, Damien, and Sam had finished packing the car just as Cassie and Alex arrived. We're gonna miss you guys so much. The three friends were commencing in a group hug. We're gonna miss you too Zozo. Cassie picked her up while referring to her nickname. Ah, for an eight-year-old, you sure are heavy. Alex joked when she had picked her up to hug her. So how long will you guys be gone? Cassie and Alex hugged Damien and Sam. Just a couple of days. Just until we stop Hunter and his Shadow Hounds. Paul loaded Max into the back of his seven-seater Land Rover. Well, I guess it's time. Paul hugged Cassie and Alex before Sarah hugged them one more time. Damien sat in the front with Paul while Sarah and Zoey rode in the back with Sam. Bye. Good luck! I hope you guys take that good for nothing jerk down. Cassie and Alex called out while waving. They watched as the car took off down the driveway before making a left turn and disappearing out of sight.

Sarah rested her head on Sam's shoulder as they made the five-hour drive to Whitebridge. Throughout their journey, they had only made two stops. They stopped at a restaurant for lunch and to take Max out to use use the bathroom. They arrived at Whitebridge around five in the afternoon. Whitebridge was a small, private town that was hidden to tourists and the public ever since the Moon's Crescent shone over their town. Whitebridge, aka wolf town, was a town inherited by wolves. People who were affected and turned into wolves by the Moon's crescent have been living there. Whitebridge is not just wolves, people who were not affected by the moon's Crescent are living there as well. Before their mother's death, Sam and Damien have been living there with Paul ever since. They drove to an old English-style house that resembled a stone cottage. This house was huge as well. Zoey wake up, we're here. Sarah gently nudged her shoulder. She yawned and rubbed her eyes. Welcome to Whitebridge. Paul parked the car. Wow, this house is beautiful. Sarah said, admiring the house. Welcome to our childhood home. Sam began to unload Max from the backseat. Yep, we have a lot of good memories here. Damien placed his hands on his hips as he looked at the house. They took the luggage into the house as they got settled in.

Chapter 21

The following moning, they had all gone into town where Paul stopped at a local hardware store to speak to his long time friend. Whitebridge was a small town so everybody knew each other. Paul! Good to see you. His friend greeted him. Its been a long time Mike. Paul responded as they stood outside the store. Ah and Damien, Sam, my have you two grown. Mike looked over at them. Hi Mr Edwards. They smiled. And who might you girls be? He noticed Sarah and Zoey. Mr Edwards, this is my girlfiend Sarah and her sister Zoey. Sam introduced. Its a pleasure to meet the both of you. He shook their hands. Paul turned to Damien and Sam. Why don't you guys go and show Sarah and Zoey around Whitebridge well Mr Edwards and I catch up? Sure. They nodded before leaving. Zoey had Max on a leash as they walked to a local cafe. This is Whitebridge cafe. They're known for their signature coffee. Best coffee in town. Damien explained as he opened the door for them, The barista looked up and noticed them before walking over to them. Hey Emma. Damien greeted. Damien? Sam? Is that really you? She hugged them. Its been ages. How are you guys? What are you doing here? She was baffled to see them. We're good. Uh, this is Sarah and Zoey. They gestued to them. Hi I'm Emma. I'm a friend of Damien and Sam's. She smiled pleasantly at them. Emma was a young nineteen year old girl. She had green eyes and long brown aurbun hair which was tied up in a ponytail. Nice to meet you Emma. Sarah smiled back. And who's this cutie pie? She bent down to pet Max. This is Max. Zoey replied. We're here because of the Moon's Crescent. Hunter Haynes returned and his after the Crescent's power. So we're trying to stop him. Damien explained. I've always hated that guy. Emma frowned. Well you're just in time, I just saw him here yesterday. Emma informed as she got up. Listen, I should get back to work but you guys are welcome to order anything you like. Its on the house. She walked back to the barista's table. Sam looked at Sarah. You gotta try their cofee, its the best. Ok, sure. I'll have a cup. Sarah smiled. Make that three. Damien ordered. And a snickerdoodle cookie for Zoey. Sam added. Coming right up. Emma chirped. She brewed the coffee and poured it in some 2 go cups, before adding sugar, milk and creamer. Then she placed three snickerdooddle cookies into some pastry bags. Here you go. Enjoy. She handed them their coffee. I snuck a little extra cookies in there for you, in case you wanted more. And here's some for you too. She murmured while handing the two bags of cookies to Sarah and Zoey. Emma's snickerdoodle cokies are the best. Once you've tried them, you're gonna keep coming back for more. Sam said. You made these? Sarah asked. That's right, I make all the cookies and pastries here. Emma replied. That's why their stuff is so good here. I remember when we were kids, I used to beg my mom to bring us here so she could get us some snickerdoodle cookies. Damien recalled. Thanks alot Emma. Yeah, thank you so much. Damien and Sarah thanked before leaving.

Damien and Sam took Sarah and Zoey to a local park that

their mom used to take them to when they were kids. They found a nice park bench that was overloking a playground. Mmm...This coffee is amazing, and it goes so well with the cookies... Sarah closed her eyes to savour the moment. I told you. Damien took a sip of his coffee. After finishing up her cookies, Zoey went to play at the playgound. They watched her climb up the ladder to the slide. Suddenly, they spotted some familiar faces coming their way. Damien and Sam got up to greet Cobalt and Toby with a bro hug. After introducing them to Sarah, they got down to business. We got your message about Hunter. The rest of the pack are here and ready to fight. Cobalt said. Good. Because the Moon's Crescent returns tonight, and we have to stop Hunter from using its power. Damien briefed. Toby and I will gather up the pack tonight, and we'll meet at Whitebridge hill. Cobalt went over the plan. Ok, sounds good. Sam and I will meet up with you guys later. Damien agreed as Cobalt and Toby left. You guys wanna grab some pizza? We know this great pizza parlour that makes the best pizza in Whitebridge. Damien insisted. Sarah was just about to answer when Zoey appeared. Sarah, I'm hungry. We were actually going to go and get some pizza. Sarah replied. The four of them walked to the pizza parlour and had odered two large pizzas. When they were done eating, they decided to get some ice cream from a parlour that the boys used to go to when they were kids. While they ate their ice cream, they walked around some more as Damien and Sam showed them more of the Whitebidge sights.

The annual Whitebridge carnival was taking place in Whitebridge that night, so Sam and Damien wanted to take Sarah and Zoey. That night around 7:00pm they arived with Paul and Max. You guys go and have fun. I'll be over there if you need me. Paul gave them money for tickets before separating with them to go and meet with his friend. Damien had Max on a leash as they made their way through the carnival. The first ride Zoey wanted to go on was the horse carousel. Seeing as she loved horses and it was her favorite ride. From there, Sarah and the boys went on the rollercoaster while Zoey stayed with Max. They went on a variety of rides including the bumper cars, kiddie swings and Sam and Sarah even went on a couple's ride on the tunnel of love before ending it with the ferris wheel. Damien and Sam had even won Sarah and Zoey some prizes by playing those tent games. Damien checked the time on his watch. Shoot. Its going for twelve, and The moon's Crescent will be taking place any minute now. We have to go. Yeah sure, Zoey and I will just stay here. I mean we are getting a little hungry, so we were thinking of grabbing some food. Sarah responded. Be careful. Just don't talk to wolves or strangers. Sam kissed her. Good luck! She called out as she watched them leave. What do you want to eat, Zo? She asked her sister. Can we get cotton candy? How about we get a hotdog first, then we can get some cotton candy? Sarah suggested. Ok, Zoey smiled before taking her sister's hand.

Hunter and his pack were already at Whitebridge hill. Our plan is coming together, father. And soon I will become the Rahu. He gazed up at the moon awaiting its transition. Its over Hunter. You don't have to do this. Damien and Sam arrived with the rest of their pack. No, you're too late, Damien. You and your mutts. Hunter shook his head. Get him! Damien yelled as he began bolting towards him. Shadow Hounds, attack! Hunter growled. Keep them back,

I need to keep still for this. Hunter ordered, while tying to push Damien away. Tony, one of the shadow wolves had pounced on Damien. It soon escalated to more wolves surrounding and pouncing on them. Meanwhile, the Moon's Crescent had began. It aluminated the moon in a blue sapphire color as it glowed and shined. Hunter stood in his wolf form, facing the moon. This is for you, father. He began chanting something. Something that was not familliar with Damien nor Sam. I don't remember any spells being involved. Damien said as he scratched a couple of wolves. Tony snarled. That's because it was all part of Hunter and Joseph's plan. Joseph knew exactly what to do and how to use the Moon's Crescent to evolve into a Rahu. Why you little... Just wait til I get my claws on you. Damien growled as he tried going for Hunter, but it was no use. The Shadow Hounds were holding them down. Cobalt and the rest of the Alpha's were pinned down by the other wolve's as well. After saying the spell, Hunter began to feel the effects. He started evolving. His legs and arms became larger, and soon after his whole body changed. He was standing on his two hind legs, his yellow eyes glowing and his black fur blowing in the wind. Yes! Finaly I have done it. I have become Rahu. He gave out a heavy, lot flat howl.

Chapter 22

Standing at ten feet tall, Hunter Haynes now a fully evolved Rahu werewolf felt proud of himself. He only wished for his father to still be here and see him. The rest of the Shadow Hounds had let go of Damien and Sam, and had gathered around Hunter. Now is our chance. Attack! Damien yelled as the Alphas charged at Hunter before pouncing on him. They used their claws to grip onto his fur, but Hunter was too strong. He pulled them off and tossed them asside. He clawed at them as he tried pushing them away. Toby, one of the Alphas had pulled on Hunter's tail, trying to pull him to the gound. But instead Hunter ended up swinging Toby around as he wagged and swung his tail. He's too strong. Huffed Sam. I know, but we have to keep trying. Damien breathed. Hunter let out a piercing roar and howl before going down on all fours and charging at the Alphas, knocking them down instantly. But they were not about to give up, they got back up and charged at him. Hunter was way bigger and stronger than them, and no matter what they did, it did'nt work. They tried scratching, and biting and griping and pulling, but nothing worked. You are no match for me, you puny little wolves. Give up well you still can. Goaded Hunter as he stared angrily at the Alphas. Dad! We need to go and find dad. He'll know what to do. Sam, go back to the carnival and find dad. Hurry! Damien instructed. Sam nodded before taking off down the hill. In the meantime, Damien and the Alphas were trying to distract Hunter and hold him off while also trying to fight off the Shadow Hounds. Sam sprinted through the trees in the forest before finding himself in civiliazation. He turned back into a human before anyone could notice and made his way in the carnival. Dad! He called out, looking different directions for him but he was nowhere to be found. Sam used his wolf smelling skills to sniff him out and could tell he nor Sarah were there. He thought of the only other place they could be, and set off for his old home. Damien and his pack were getting tired but did'nt want to give up. Alpha pack, hunting formation! Go! Go! Damien ordered. The Alphas did what they were told as they began using their hunting strategy on the other wolves. Half of the pack circled Hunter while the others circled the Shadow pack. They began doing what they normally do to prey, when they go hunting as a pack. They circled Hunter and the wolves before herding and finally cornering them somewhere. Sam arrived at the house as he shapeshifted back into a human and knocked on the door. When Paul answered the door, he was surprised to see his son. Dad, we need your help to stop Hunter. Long story short, he's evolved. He quickly briefed. Sam? You had me worried. What going on? Sarah came from the living room and hugged him. No time to explain. I'm kinda in a hurry. I know exactly how you can stop Hunter. Sarah, where is that book I gave you? Paul turned to her. The book on the Moon's Crescent? She asked. He nodded. Hang on a sec. She disappeared up the stairs before returning momenterilly with the book and handing it to Paul. He skimmed through the pages and stopped at a page on how to stop a fully evolved Rahu wolf. Here, read this spell and it will permanetly take away Hunter's powers, and make him mortal. But the whole wolf pack has to read the spell or it will not work. Paul explained as he read what was in the book. Ok, thanks. Sam turned into a wolf again before taking the book with his mouth. Paul held the door open for him as he sprinted back to Whitebridge hill.

Meanwhile, Damien and the rest of his pack were struggling to take down Hunter and his wolves. Their hunting tactic did'nt work. Kill them! All of them! Hunter's voice was deep and low. Where are you Sam? Damien mumbled. I don't think we can win this fight. We're too tired. Toby said while he and Damien looked around to see their pack members panting from exhaustion. Just then, Sam appeared still holding the book in his mouth. He placed the book on the ground and told Damien what his dad had told him. I knew dad would figure something out. Where's Sarah and Zoey? Damien asked. They're back home with dad. Sam responded, transforming into a human and flipping through the pages of the book. Good. They need to be in a safe place right now. Damien said. Found it. Sam placed the book on the ground and once again, turned back into a wolf. Damien called his pack into a huddle and told them the plan. They lined up next to each other and faced Hunter and is wolves. Listen up, Shadows. You may think you won this time. But you did'nt. You lost. Big time. This is our terf and we're not gonna let you guys take it and ruin it. So we just have one thing to say. Damien addresed them. Are you surrendering already? I did'nt think you had the guts. Hunter started laughing. By the powers of Day and the powers of Night, bring protection here this night. The moon is full, the sky is clear, misfortune and evil disappear. The mighty wolf should ever reign and be protected from harm and bane. Spirits of the wolf, strong and great! Be guarded by this circle and the power of the moon's crescent. Damien and the Alphas started chanting the spell from the book. They said it at least three times as the full moon above glowed in its sapphire color. It illuminated a bright ray of light and shoned over Hunter. He began to levitate off the ground as it lifed him up and proceeded to work its magic on him. What's happening to me? Hunter fretted as his body began to tingle. Shortly after, he started descending and was brought back down. He realized he was back to his normal self as he looked at his arms and his bare chest before feeling his blonde hair. What the hell did you and your pack do to me? Hunter rebuked. We changed you back into a human. Permanently. You're not going to be a wolf anytime soon. Your days of being a wolf, is over. Damien felt satisfied now that Hunter was finally defeated. Freeze! Don't move! Two police officers had arrived, pointing their guns at Hunter. They were not acting scared when they saw the wolves around him. Dad must of called them. Sam murmured. The officers handcuffed him and led him away.

Chapter 23

The news of Hunter Haynes getting arrested surprised the residents of Whitebridge. They were glad Hunter had been stopped and taken away for good. It was like a weight had been lifted off their shoulders. Everyone was gathered outside the city hall building as the mayor addressed them. This town has been tormented by Hunter Haynes for ten years now, and last night he did the unthinkable. He evolved himself into what we know a Rahu wolf. If it weren't for a couple of brave wolves, Hunter would have probably killed half this town. But we are very grateful for those wolves who stood up and fought. Even though they got injured doing it, they are heroes to Whitebridge. So I came up with a little solution that could help Whitebridge. The mayor continued. We have put together a pack of wolves who have agreed to watch over and protect this town from people like Hunter Haynes. I give you the Wolves of Whitebridge. He gestured to a group of young boys and girls. Everyone applauded and cheered when the mayor had finished. Emma turned to face Damien, Sam, and Sarah. Are you guys sure you can't stick around a little longer? Nah, we need to get back to Chesterfield and finish our senior year of high school. Damien replied. I'm sure gonna miss you guys. Emma hugged them before crouching down to hug Zoey. How about some coffee and cookies for the road? You know it. Sam smiled. Be right back. Emma made her way through the crowd. Well, I don't know how you boys did it, but you did it. You freed this town from a burden and we are eternally grateful. Mike gave them a pat on the back as he hugged Sam and Damien. Paul gave his friend one last hug just as Emma returned with the coffee and cookies. Thanks again, Emma. I will always remember these. Sarah chuckled. Well. I wrote down the recipe for my snickerdoodle cookies so you could always have them wherever you are. She smiled. Thank you. Sarah hugged her again. Whenever you're in Chesterfield, look us up. The four of them got into the car with Paul and pulled out from their parking space. They waved back to Mike and Emma who were watching them leave.

Cassie and Alex have been waiting for them at the Abbot house for a few hours now. They were sitting in Cassie's car applying lipstick to their lips. They looked through the rearview mirror and saw the reflection of Paul's black Land Rover. They're back! They're back! Alex screamed in excitement as the girls got out of the car. As soon as Paul parked the car, Sarah quickly got out and threw herself into their arms. The three girls screamed as they embraced. Zoey! Alex picked her up, and after embracing her she handed her to Cassie. We missed you guys so much. Cassie wrapped her arms around Zoey, almost squeezing her. We were only gone for like three days. Damien stated. Damien! Cassie jumped into his arms. He chuckled while wrapping his arms around her. I missed you too, Cass. He kissed her before placing her on the ground again. After getting their stuff and their luggage, they told Alex and Cassie everything that had happened in Whitebridge. Damn, that must have been scary. Alex said. It was, but we took

Hunter down and he's in prison now. Now let's just forget about him and celebrate our return. Damien grinned. Right ahead of you son. Paul smiled. They ordered pizza and watched a couple of movies.

After celebrating and spending time with one another, Sam and Damien wanted to speak to Sarah about something serious. Sarah, there's something Sam and I have been wanting to talk to you about. Damien began as they sat next to her on the couch. What is it? She asked, rather concerned. Do you want to be a wolf? They questioned. What? She gave them a puzzled look. Would you like to be a wolf? I can turn you into one if you want. Sam looked at her. Seriously. you can do that? Cassie was shocked. Paul nodded in response. That's right, wolves have the power to turn a human into a wolf just by scratching them. What would this mean for me then? Sarah queried. You will just be a wolf like us. You can join our pack meetings and be an Alpha. Sam explained. Sarah looked over at her friends. What about them? They can be wolves too. I mean if they want to. Damien looked at Cassie and Alex who were seated on another couch. If Sarah's going to become a wolf, so will I. Cassie stood up. Yeah, me too. I think we should do this together. I mean we are best friends, right? Alex stood up next to Cassie. Sarah took a deep breath. Ok, let's do it. Let's be wolves. Can I be a wolf too? Zoey asked. No, there's no way that I'm letting you be a wolf. Sorry, Zo. Sarah replied as Sam took her hand and held it out so that her palm was facing up. Are you sure you guys wanna do this? Damien and Sam looked at the girls again. They nodded. We are. Sam rubbed his thumb on her palm before transforming his hand into a wolf's claw. He began to insert one of his claws on her palm and scratched her downwards, leaving a laceration. Ouch! She squirmed and closed her eyes at the feeling. When he was done, she saw the blood run down her palm as she clenched it into a fist. Who's next? Damien asked.

It will take some time for you guys to get used to it. But in the meantime, Sam and I will show you the ropes and teach you how to be wolves. There's a wolf council meeting in the forest tonight, and you guys are coming with us. I'm sure the rest of the pack will be glad to meet you. Damien briefed. Before leaving that night, Sarah, Cassie, and Alex were able to transform into three beautiful white wolves with fur as white as snow, and shimmering eyes. So, how do I look? Cassie asked. Her blue eyes sparkling. Pretty. I-I mean you all look pretty. Damien responded, kind of in a daze. Would you look at that? White wolves. Marveled Paul. Sarah, you look amazing. Sam was dumbfounded when he saw her. Thanks. She smiled. The girls took a quick look in the mirror and couldn't believe what they saw. Wow, is that really me? Sarah was just flabbergasted. What do you think Zoey? She looked at her sister for a comment. Whoah, you guys look really cool. I can't believe I'm a wolf. Cassie was still trying to process it. We should get going. The meeting starts in a few minutes. Damien said. The five of them made their way to their regular meeting place in the forest. Damien, Sam, hey. Cobalt greeted. Who are you, friends? He asked when he saw the three white wolves. Guys, we'd like for you to meet Sarah Cooper, Cassie Andrews and Alex Pierce, the newest members of the Alpha Hounds. Damien introduced them. Welcome aboard. Cobalt nodded. Now I want to start this meeting off by saying that I've decided to elect a new member to become our

leader for the Alphas. He climbed onto some rocks. Damien Abbot. He's not only our friend, but a renowned leader. His dignity and bravery is what stopped Hunter and his pack. He is resourcefull and he never gives up even when times are tough. He knows how to put up a fight, and for those reasons, I nominate Damien as our new leader. Cobalt addressed. Thanks, man. Damien got on the rock that Cobalt was standing on. Thanks guys for making me your new pack leader. Together, we're gonna take this pack to the top. He howled before the others joined in.
When the meeting ended, Toby had approached Alex. Hey, I'm Toby, Toby Brian. He introduced himself. I'm Alex. She spoke shyly. Its a nice night out and I was wondering if you wanted to go for a walk with me? He offered. Sure. I'd love to. Alex smiled. Sam and Sarah were frolicking in the forest together. They started playing and chasing each other, as Sam managed to pin her to the ground. And at that moment, they gazed into each other's eyes. Her golden brown eyes glowing in the dark. While gazing, Sarah could'nt help herself but lick him on the cheek. They got up and rubbed against each other. Meanwhile, Damien and Cassie were taking a walk themselves. Sam, Sarah, Damien, Cassie, Toby and Alex all walked into school together Monday morning. They were all holding hands with their significant other. Sarah was not your basic average girl anymore, she was a wolf and an Alpha Hound. She was even dating a super cute wolf. But she was'nt alone, she had her two best friends by her side. Who knows what she'll get herself into next.

www.ingramcontent.com/pod-product-compliance
Lightning Source LLC
LaVergne TN
LVHW050420160726
843469LV00041B/1169

* 9 7 8 9 3 5 6 1 0 8 3 1 8 *